Think of the c   .. rainbow's end
... just after the dawn
... listen
... as they sing a joyful song
... they carry the tune
... to this side of the moon
it is here the song remains
WHAT A GLORIOUS SOUND HOPE IS
there is no sickness
... no tears are shed
for these children
... a life
... fringed with hope
... has just begun
in this place... not so far from view
... meant only for a special few

Think of the children at the rainbow's end
... when the brightness of the sun... warms your flesh
... ignites the flame within your soul
while the children chase porcelain clowns
... up and down
... and all around
WHAT A GLORIOUS SOUND HOPE IS
in this place... not so far from view
... meant only for a special few

Think of a parent at the rainbow's end
... when moon beams tap dance... here and there
... ride the waves
... chase the tide
even under an enchanted moon
... a mother has no where to hide
so she places her fears in a mermaid's hands
... until they fade away
... beneath the sea
for there is nothing she wouldn't do
... to ease her child's pain
it's that time again
... to find that place... not so far from view
... meant only for a special few
WHAT A GLORIOUS SOUND HOPE IS

Think of the children at the rainbow's end
... when human decency hangs in the balance
... and the magician fumbles
... and the puppet fails to answer the simplest command
for there is no where to hide
... even under an enchanted moon
wishes are granted only to a special few
on this side of the moon... not so far from view
WHERE THE GLORIOUS SOUND OF HOPE CAN BE HEARD
sung by the children at the rainbow's end

Judy Ortado

Dedicated to Linda Angelone... a true angel

Foreward:

"WHO CARES WHAT MOST ANGEL'S DO"

WHEN ASKED TO WRITE THIS FOREWARD
BLOWN AWAY I GOTTA SAY
THE DAY THAT I MET JUDY
GOD HUMBLED ME THAT DAY

WHO CARES WHAT MOST ANGEL'S DO
IS THE TITLE OF HER BOOK
I HOPE EVERYONE TAKES TIME
TO OPEN IT..& TAKE A LOOK

HER JOURNEY STARTED YEARS AGO
AFTER CANCER TOOK HER DAD
LINDA FROM RAINBOW'S HOPE
HELPED HEAL SORROW, JUDY HAD

JUDY OFFERED HER WRITINGS
& ALSO GAVE YOU HER HEART
TO ANY CHILD OR PARENT
NEEDING A VOICE TO PLAY A PART

IT WAS THEN THAT SHE MET DOLLY
WHO WORKED BY LINDA'S SIDE
JUDY WAS GIVEN 2 ANGELS
IN HER LIFE... ON THIS RIDE

JUDY WROTE THIS STORY
FOR CHILDREN TO HAVE HOPE
ILLUSTRATIONS DONE BY THEM
THEIR ANGELS TO HELP THEM COPE

THE CHILDREN DREW THESE ANGELS
TO MIMIC THEIR OWN VIEWS
THEY WERE GIVEN FREEDOM
TO DRAW THEM AS THEY CHOOSE

THE CHILDREN HELD THEIR CRAYONS
& COLORED THE WORLD WITH HOPE
THROUGH GOD & ALL HIS GLORY
IN HELPING THESE CHILDREN COPE

JUDY SEES REFLECTIONS
IN A CHILD'S EYES
VISIONS OF GOD'S ANGELS
SOOTHING CHILDREN'S CRIES

ANGELICA IS THE ANGEL
WHO LIVES WITHIN THIS BOOK
SHE SOFTENS ALL THE ILLNESS
FOR FAMILIES IT SHOOK

ONE DAY WHEN JUDY MEETS THE LORD
HE WILL SMILE AT HER & SAY
YOU HELPED A CHILD'S SPIRIT GROW
IN HEAVEN, YOU'RE WELCOMED TODAY!

GOD BLESS YOU,
GERI PETITO

4 A STAR Publishing
75 Iroquois Dr.
Galloway, NJ 08205
www.4astar.com/publishing

Every once in a lifetime, or so they say, an angel falls from the sky
... in an extraordinary way.
First comes the blackness... next...the clouds surround the sun...
Each star in the Universe loses its glimmer... one... by one... by one.

As fast as lightning... as fast as can be... that very Angel falls
... down... down... down...
to the very bottom of the sea.
Still, this doesn't seem likely. Angels have wings.
They are beautiful and mystical...
... And other glorious things.

Angels are spiritual beings... images in white...
They wear golden halos...
That glisten in the night.
They are willowy and radiant, dazzling and true.
Angels are neon and opal... and oh, so heavenly, too.

They are gentle and innocent. They are topaz and pearls.
Come to think of it, are angels boys or are they girls?
Are their eyes blue... or brown, hazel... or green?
Is paradise the only place they have ever seen?

Are Angels big or are they small?
And what if an Angel really did fall?
I guess it could happen, you know...
every once in a lifetime, that is...
if they say so.

Ernie

8 years

Just like Angelica... an Angel with a broken wing...
with a sweet sounding name...
without a song to sing.
It was her lovely melody that once filtered through the skies,
that echoed through the darkness...
when you closed your eyes.

For it was Angelica who sang the saintly tune...
that put you to sleep from July through June...
And Angelica who fell all the way down... down... down...
in her gossamer gown.

It happened so quickly. It was quite a surprise.
Angelica tripped over a star... and right before her eyes
... the sky opened... and she bumped her wing
... on the sun... no... the moon...
OH... SHE BUMPED IT ON SOMETHING.

Nevertheless, she had no time to lose
... so she grabbed her halo and her sapphire shoes...
And before she knew it...
in the blink of an eye... down... down... down...
she fell, from that hole in the sky.

Jessica
Age 4½

She started to count, but before she reached three,
there she was... at the very bottom of the sea.
For even Angels are breakable... just like you and me.
Sometimes things don't turn out...
the way we would like them to be.

So we must either flow with the tides...
or follow the sun... or reach for the stars...
There's a RAINBOW deep inside everyone.
And most important of all ... there is always HOPE.
And that is the one gift that helps,
even Angels to cope.

Maybe Angelica's wing will never mend,
but that doesn't mean
Happiness has come to an end.
As long as there's at least one WISH in her heart...
That's how new beginnings get their start.

And if her wish isn't granted,
She can make a new wish.
If she can't fly like an Angel,
Why can't she swim like a fish?
If Angels can fly, they can swim, too?
WHO CARES IF FLYING IS WHAT MOST ANGELS DO.

Diane

I am 7

angel

and

said

Why can't Angels make a whirlpool?
... Or backstroke here and there.
There's no need to glide through the cloud...
unless there are clouds around somewhere.
For even Angels are breakable... just like you and me.
Sometimes things don't turn out the way we would like them to be.

Yet the lovely melody that once filtered through the skies...
that echoed through the darkness when you closed your eyes...
that Angelica sang...the saintly tune... that put you to sleep...
from July through June...
... Can still be heard... only now it's a different song...
that ripples through the ocean all night long.

For Angels are forever willowy and radiant, dazzling and true...
Neon and opal... and oh, so heavenly too.
Who know, Angelica may learn to love
the very bottom of the sea.
Even a broken Angel, can be the best Angel she can be.

There may be Angels from other lifetimes
down there to keep her company.
And maybe next time, Angelica will watch
where she's going
just between you and me !!!

Judy Ortado

Author's Note:

"WHO CARES WHAT MOST ANGELS DO" is the culmination of all that is precious in this life of ours. Each stroke of crayon is a ray of sunlight… in a World where the Sun fails us from time to time. It is the spirit of HOPE. It is a child stricken with catastrophic illness…grasping on to a single magical thread that dangles from the inner soul. A place few of us will witness...

... A place darkened by pain and confusion.
... A place where miracles are sorely needed.

On each page of this book there is a longing. A desire so strong for a bright future.
... Rays of sunlight so vivid. And yet, only a select few will see the
   beauty that lies within.

" WHO CARES WHAT MOST ANGELS DO " is a rainbow, colored with COMPASSION.

... It is a serenade.
... It is a child riding the waves of a magical ocean…
... Climbing into a fairytale ..
... Holding the reins of a mythical horse on a carousel.

 Most of all, .it is a gift of LOVE.

... Drawn by the hands of Angels…
... Nurtured by those who call to the Angels for all that is precious in this
   life of ours.
... Meant for the select few who wish to see the beauty that lies within.

Judy Ortado
judy.angelbook@gmail.com